KT-552-108

THIS WALKER BOOK BELONGS TO:

Harry,
Love Sacha
x x x

For Harry who inspired it. M.W.

For Willie who found a good friend. B.F.

First published 2003 by Walker Books Ltd, 87 Vauxhall Walk, London SE11 5HJ
This edition published 2004   10 9 8 7 6 5 4 3 2 1
Text © 2003 Martin Waddell   Illustrations © 2003 Barbara Firth
The right of Martin Waddell and Barbara Firth to be identified as author
and illustrator respectively of this work has been asserted by them
in accordance with the Copyright, Designs and Patents Act 1988
This book has been typeset in Godlike   Printed in China
All rights reserved   British Library Cataloguing
in Publication Data: a catalogue record for
this book is available from the British Library
ISBN 0-7445-9847-8   www.walkerbooks.co.uk

HI, HARRY!

Martin Waddell

illustrated by

Barbara Firth

WALKER BOOKS
AND SUBSIDIARIES
LONDON · BOSTON · SYDNEY · AUCKLAND

Harry Tortoise

sat on his tree-stump.

He wanted
to play,

but he had no one
to play with.

Along came Buster Rabbit.

"Hi, Buster!" said Harry.
"Can I play with you?"

"Can't stop. Got to keep going!"
Buster called.

"Going where?"
Harry asked.

But Buster
had gone.

Stan Badger came by.
"Hi, Stan!" said Harry.

"Can't talk just now!"
Stan called.

"Why not?"
Harry asked.

But Stan Badger
had gone.

Along came Sarah Mouse.
"Hi, Sarah!" said Harry.

"I've got to hop. Mustn't
be late!" Sarah said.

"Late for what?"
Harry asked.

But Sarah Mouse
wasn't there any more.

I wish I had someone to play with, thought Harry.

Someone not quick who has time to play with a tortoise.

Harry set off . . .

so slow slow

. . . . slowly

to find someone
to play with.

"Hi, Mushroom,"
said Harry.

"Hi, Rock,"
said Harry.

"Hi, Pool,"
said Harry.

"Hi, Harry,"
said Harry to Harry.

"Hi, Harry!"
said someone.

"Who said that?" gasped Harry.

"It was me," said Sam Snail. "Can I play with you, Harry?"

"YES!"
Harry said.

They played Slow Races.

Heads In and . . .

Heads Out.

Turn Around and . . .

Turn Around Back Again.

Then they sat by the pool and they talked and talked about being a tortoise and being a snail, about tree-stumps and puddles, and mushrooms and moss, and the trouble with rabbits and badgers and mice . . .

and how good
it is to be
slow.

And how nice, how very very very nice, it is to be . . . friends.

WALKER BOOKS is the world's leading independent publisher of children's books. Working with the best authors and illustrators we create books for all ages, from babies to teenagers – books your child will grow up with and always remember. So...

FOR THE BEST CHILDREN'S BOOKS, LOOK FOR THE BEAR